CATWAD

IT'S ME.

CATWAD

IT'S ME.

JIM BENTON

graphix AN IMPRINT OF
SCHOLASTIC

5

7

14

HEY, DING-DONG. I'M PRETTY SURE YOU READ THAT WRONG. THAT WOULD BE **WAY** TOO LONG.

CATWAD, CAN WE PLEASE HAVE THIS CONVERSATION **AFTER** I BRUSH MY TEETH?

WORKS FOR ME.

25

37

38

39

43

WHAT ARE YOU WASTING YOUR TIME ON NOW?

I'M WORKING ON A NEW WAY TO SIGN MY NAME

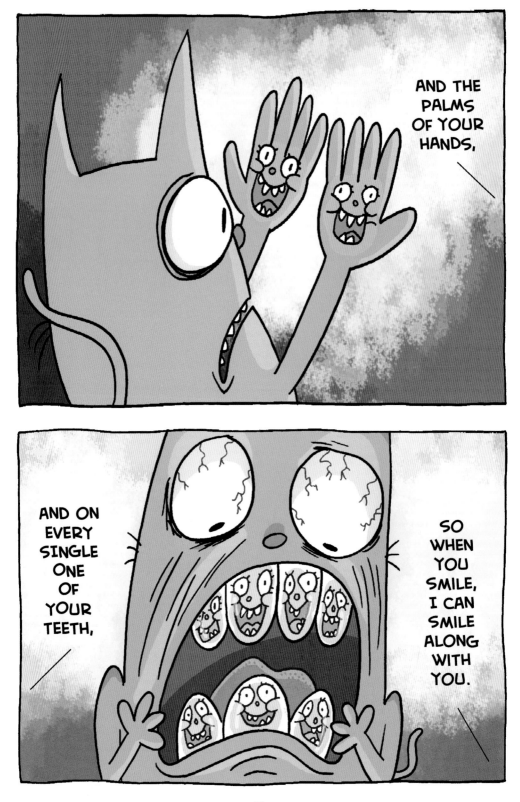

WELL, IT'S OVER NOW,
SO DON'T WORRY ABOUT IT.
AND BESIDES, I DID
SOMETHING THAT'S
GONG TO MAKE YOU
**REALLY, REALLY,
HAPPY...**

OH YEAH?
WHAT WAS IT?

Well, I *thought about* being one of those mysterious and ANGRY HEROES OF THE NIGHT.

But my bedtime is too early for that.

I considered getting bitten by some RADIOACTIVE BUG.

But I was afraid it might be one of those dumb bugs that just crawls around on *dog poo.*

And I couldn't be one of those guys that gets BIG AND STRONG when he gets angry.

Because getting big and strong would make me so happy that I would just *shrink* again.

Unicorns, as you know, are the most beautiful living things in the world, and Fairies are the most magical.

Legend tells us of a tiny creature with the pointy horn of A Unicorn, and the lovely, delicate Wings of A Fairy.

The story says on enchanted nights like this, if you're very, very, lucky, one of them might even land on you and kiss you with his horn.

69

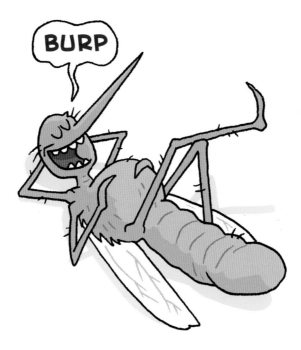

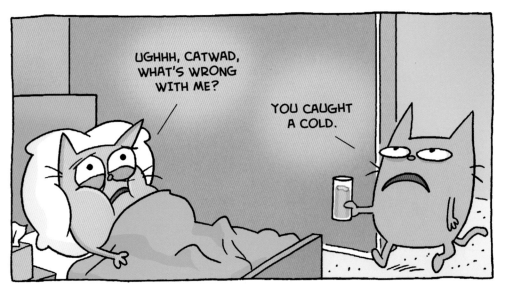

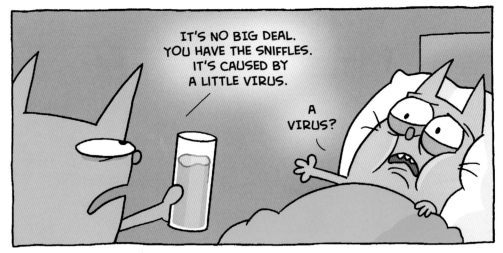

AND A FEW MORE THINGS... EVERYTHING HAS TO BE PERFECTLY CLEAN FOR BABIES EVEN THOUGH THEY LIKE TO THROW UP ON THEMSELVES AND SIT AROUND IN DIRTY DIAPERS.

AND WE CAN'T HAVE ANYTHING SHARP SHE COULD HURT HERSELF WITH OR STUFF SHE COULD ACCIDENTALLY SWALLOW LIKE GUM OR DYNAMITE.

AND I DON'T WANT HER TO SEE ANYTHING TOO SCARY, LIKE ZOMBIE MOVIES OR MY GRANDMA'S GIANT UNDERPANTS.

AND ALSO I WANT TO... MAKE...SURE..THAT...

ZZZZZZZZZZ

HAPPY MOTHER'S DAY
Love, your ♥ Virus

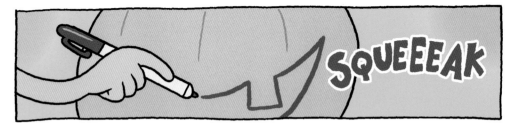

SQUEEEAK

CATWAD! COME HERE AND LOOK AT MY JOLLY **JACK-O-LANTERN.**

LOOK! I DREW A BIG HAPPY FACE TO CUT OUT.

LET'S SEE HOW LONG HE FEELS HAPPY...

97

111

112

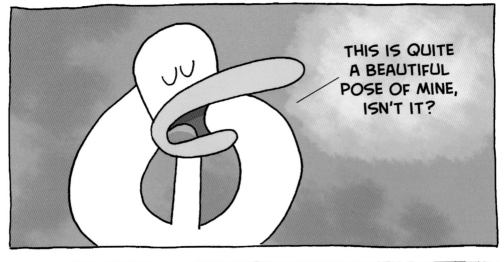

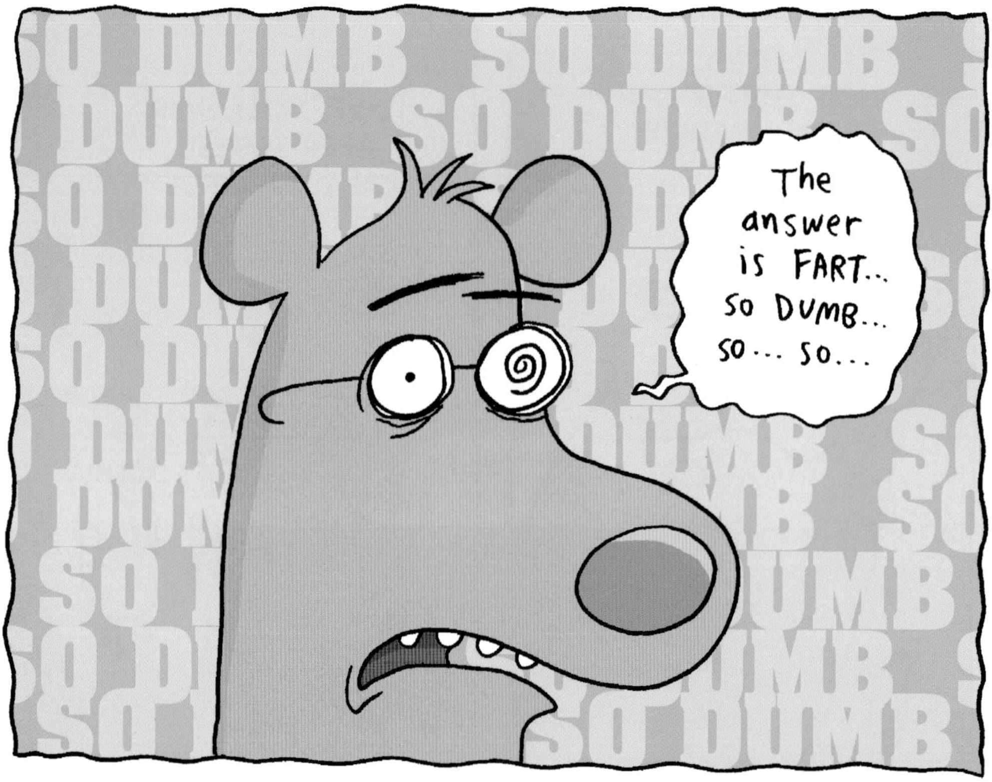
SO DUMB SO DUMB
The answer is FART... SO DUMB... SO... SO...

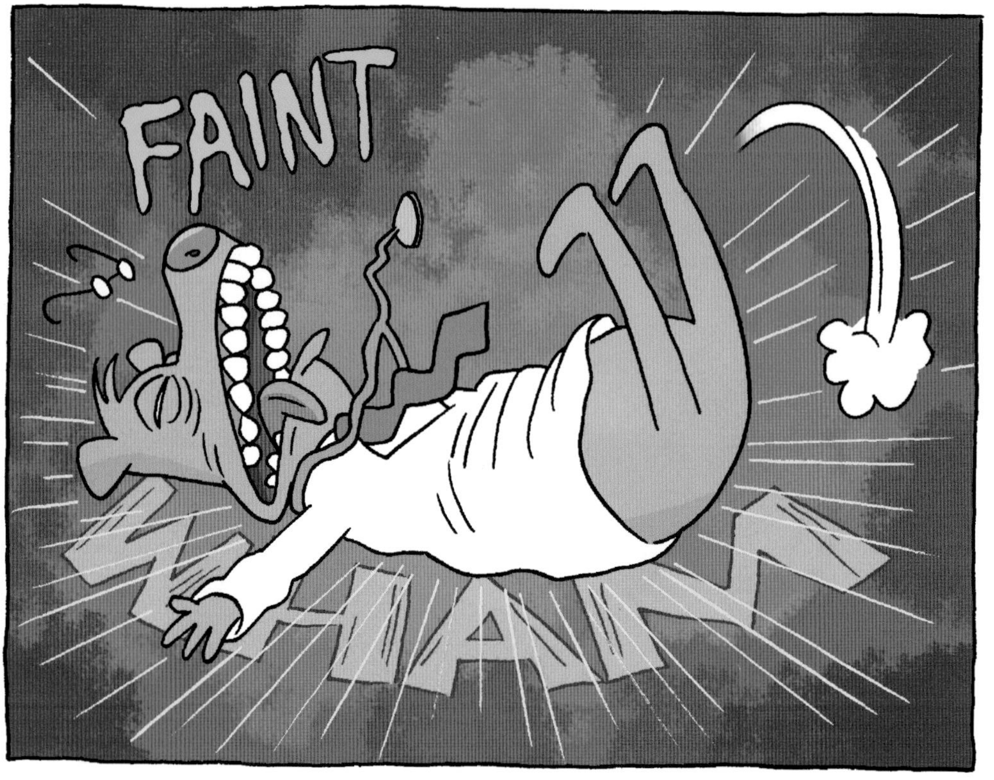
FAINT
WHAM

BREAKING NEWS-
Witnesses are
reporting that
Dumbness has
broken out
all over the
country.

A number of victims have come
down with dumb-itis after having
contact with one individual.

Police have
released this
sketch of the
individual.

125

CATWAD- CAN YOU HEAR ME? ARE YOU OK?
POOF
I ASKED YOU ABOUT VITAMIN C AND YOU JUST WENT BLANK.
LIBRARY
MAKE TIME TO READ!
WHAT ARE WE DOING HERE?
SAVING THE WORLD.
DON'T MISS CATWAD #2!

BONUS ACTIVITY!
CAN YOU FIND THE TWO IDENTICAL BLURMPS?